W9-BVT-828

Ramar was shivering
as he left the warmth
of the World-In-Between.

He drifted, then soared,
then drifted again while
the heat of the sun beat
down on his shoulders.
But still he trembled as
he searched through the
clouds for the Earth below.

What difference could he
make to a world, he wondered,
so different from his own?
What could a rabbit with
rainbow wings know
of love or of wisdom
or the meaning of life?

What could he say that
The Shepherd had not said
when he was there?
Or what could he know that had
not been known to Muhammad or
Buddha or to all of the prophets
come down through the ages?

But then, once born, he would
no longer be a rabbit. He would
be a child of the Earth. His rainbow
wings would be gone and forgotten . . .
a part of that World-In-Between
he was leaving behind with those
who loved him. His wings and
maybe his memories, too.

The thought alarmed him.

"Please, Shepherd!" he cried to himself,
"don't let me forget why I've come to be born."

Then . . . as if in answer, the clouds parted beneath him,
and there below, in the bright summer sun, stretched
the oceans and lands of Earth, and he felt himself pulled
across them to a small gray house next to a
schoolyard where children played.

He knew that in this modest house, in a bedroom behind the kitchen,
his mother awaited his birth. Her pains were quickening now,
coming closer and closer together, and she cried aloud.

He knew it was time. He knew he was home.

Ramar

THE RABBIT WITH RAINBOW WINGS

DARRELL T. HARE

St. Martin's Press

New York

RAMAR: THE RABBIT WITH RAINBOW WINGS.

Copyright © 1996 by Darrell T. Hare and The Wizards, Inc. All rights reserved. Printed in the United States of America. No part of this book may be used or reproduced in any manner whatsoever without written permission except in the case of brief quotations embodied in critical articles or reviews. For information, write St. Martin's Press, 175 Fifth Avenue, New York, N.Y. 10010.

Book design copyright © by Joan Stoliar
Illustrations copyright © by Tom O'Sullivan
Title calligraphy copyright © by Jeanyee Wong

Book design by Joan Stoliar

AN ELEANOR FRIEDE BOOK

Library of Congress Cataloging-in-Publication Data
Hare, Darrell T.
Ramar: The rabbit with rainbow wings / Darrell T. Hare — 1st ed.
P.   cm.
"An Eleanor Friede Book" — T.p. verso.
ISBN 0-312-14031-2
I. Title.
PS3558.A624142R36   1996
813'.54 -- dc20   95-45190   CIP

First Edition: March 1996
10 9 8 7 6 5 4 3 2 1

RAMAR is a story of rare and lasting friendship and so it is dedicated to my good and gifted friends Wendell Larson, Eleanor Friede, Steve Lake, and Robert Englert.

RAMAR is also a story of loving support and so it is written for every person who loves and supports another, but especially for my family — Marilyn, Randy, Cynthia, Brittany, Tim, Amy and Adam.

Finally, RAMAR is a story of learning through love and so it is written for those from whom I have learned the longest—my twin brother Dale, my big brother John, and most of all my mother, Ermal Hare Arnold, who unknowingly taught me to believe in such things as courage and kindness and rabbits with wings.

One

My memory of Ramar begins long before his journey to Earth. It goes back through a loop of time and space to a place so distant from me now that I sometimes question I was ever there . . . but the doubting is rare and lasts for just a moment.

I see it too clearly for that.

The trees, I recall, are strong and tall, and the land is aglow with the same golden browns that shine on Earth. You can lie upon it on summer days and dream your dreams. And beyond the land, where the mountains rise to hide the moon, the sky is a glorious blue, and there when the sounds of night grow quiet, you can hear the songs of distant creatures as they wing their way homeward.

I think of it now as an in-between place, a world that is not a world in a time that is not a time. Yet I know it is there, as real as the memory of Ramar, whose life I record on these pages. So I will write as I remember.

When Ramar first appeared, it was a bright Spring day like the kind we know on Earth when the bushes have begun to leaf and the night holds threat of frost, not yet done with the winter.

Ramar was not born in the way we think of birth. It was more as though someone had crystallized a thought and the thought took form as a rabbit, alive and asleep in the end of a hollow log, his face nuzzled warmly between his paws and his nose in a lively twitch.

It was early morning, and at the sound of a robin's first song, Ramar awoke and stretched himself full length. He yawned and washed his face with the moisture on his tongue, and looked around him. He knew inside that he had come alive for the very first time, awake in a world he did not know but where he somehow belonged.

Yes, I remember more perfectly now.

The place where I came to know Ramar is in a world where all of us live between the times we spend on Earth. It is a place, as I have said, not so much different from the world around us here. It is we who are different in the times we spend there. Our hearts are warmer. Our minds are open and more perceptive, and our spirits grow through the bonds we share with one another. The things we feel are stronger, too — stronger and truer than the things we think most times.

Ramar knew this the instant he opened his eyes.

He knew what living is, and what he felt was a smile inside, a joy in taking a breath, of knowing, of being, of feeling all the gifts that were his to know.

"Alive!" he thought. "I am really alive!" And feeling the miracle of that, he gave a kick that rabbits give when they first discover joy.

Somehow, though, even in the happiness he felt, he sensed there was something different about him. It was something that set him apart from every other rabbit who had ever existed. He knew he had wings, tiny wisps of gossamer that grew from his shoulders, the color of the earth upon which he rested. He could not see them. He could not touch them. All he could do was to know they were there.

So that is how Ramar began his life — as a small winged rabbit in a world that you and I, except in our dreams, have all but forgotten. He had a heart he could feel with, a mind he could think with, and an eagerness to learn what few but a child could understand.

The marvelous thing was that Ramar intuitively knew that life is a gift that is infinitely precious. It is a gift so great that even if you are different, and others laugh to see you, it makes no matter. It is only the gift that matters, it and the part of ourselves that we learn to give to others.

Ramar understood this right away, and as he grew in that gold-green meadow, he gave little thought to the wings he carried or the reason for their being. He found instead a certain oneness with everything that grew and flew about him, and with all that he saw and touched. The blades of grass beneath his toes, the roots of the trees. The hawthorn, the hills, and the hummingbirds. They were all a part of him, it seemed, and he of them . . . with a language between them that was never spoken, and bonds that held them together but left them free to grow apart.

Ramar in his way, and they in theirs.

I could hear him, too, in my own rabbit-heart, and every so often, I would chase along behind him through the fields and thickets. I would hear his laughter then, calling back to me, and I would smile at the sound of its singing.

Ramar loved the sun and how it warmed him, so much so that on days when the clouds grew close together and the light disappeared for awhile, he would forget his play and lie in his log alone, thinking thoughts that no one could hear.

I knew then that Ramar was not different just because of his wings. He was different because of what he was, and knew, and heard inside himself. It was a voice inside his own, and it spoke to him in his quiet times as he drifted to sleep. The choice was his to listen or not or to follow what he heard.

One thing he knew was that he was not alone in the World-In-Between.

Except for humans, there were creatures of every sort. Elephants and sparrows. Ants and giraffes. Lizards and lions. Tigers and toads. There were none, however, that Ramar could describe as his friend until one day near the start of his second Summer.

That's when Lydia came.

It was clear to Ramar from the instant he saw her that Lydia was a cat of unusual splendor. It was something in her eyes, he felt. No, it was more than that. It was all of her, the way she carried herself when she walked, the gentle and patient way she spoke . . . or more correctly, the way she didn't speak. She simply thought, it seemed, and Ramar heard the words inside his head as though they were words of his own.

Whatever it was about her, she won Ramar over with just a smile. "I am Lydia," she said, "and I have heard all about you. The rabbit with the gossamer wings."

Ramar smiled and lowered his head. He could not decide how to answer.

"I have come to be your friend," said Lydia, "your friend and your teacher, if you will let me help you."

Ramar tried to say hello but nothing came out, just the word in his mind. But Lydia heard him and smiled. "That is how friends communicate," she told him. "You just think what you want to say and I will hear you, the same as you hear me."

"Is that how everyone talks?" asked Ramar.

"Well, everyone and everything," Lydia replied. "It is not just creatures who speak with each other. Everything has a language. You can talk with the wind. You can talk with the rocks and the river. You can talk with everything around you if you learn how to listen."

"You mean everything can hear me?" asked Ramar. "Every rock and every tree and . . . everything?"

"No," said Lydia. "Only the things you feel part of or let inside your heart. That is the secret . . . the feelings you have between you."

Ramar smiled. It was good to have Lydia to talk with. She was everything at the same time. She was young. She was old. She was warm. She was wise. She felt close and comfortable as though she and Ramar had lived in each other's hearts for centuries before. Centuries he could not remember.

"All of us here have lived forever," Lydia told him. "It is only you who is new among us. You have not yet been born as a human being or lived in the world as a person."

"A person?" Ramar asked.

"Every creature you see around you," Lydia explained, "has lived as a person on a place we call Earth. It is not a faraway world. It is just a different kind of existence than we experience here . . . as different, say, as dreaming is from waking."

Then Ramar remembered. "I have had dreams of that world!" he shouted.

The dreams had come about every night while Ramar slept, and each of them took him on a journey to Earth, where he would walk among the people who lived there. The dreams were not frightening because the Earth seemed like a natural place for him to be. He was somehow at home, a part of that world and those within it, and yet apart from it, too.

The trouble was that when Ramar awoke, the dreams disappeared before he could catch them and etch them in his mind. The journeys. The people. The cities he saw. They always escaped him when he opened his eyes, and he rarely got them back except for a glimmer or two in moments when he did not expect them.

"Dreams are like that," said Lydia. "They let you catch glimpses of other times and other worlds so you know that you are not alone or held to the place where you are."

"Have you been a human before?" asked Ramar.

"Many, many times," said Lydia, "many more times than I can tell you."

She had been a queen, she remembered, in the thirteenth century, and a warrior before that. A sailor, too. Then once a poet and once a priest. A teacher, a scholar, a mother, a monk. All her lives seemed as one to her now, each but a fleeting moment in an ocean of time and space.

Some she remembered. Some she did not.

The one thing she knew above all was that to grow in grace and spirit, she had to live all the experiences a person could live and in all the ways she could live them. She had to see and feel and touch all that life could be.

Above all, as every worthy spirit must, no matter what hardship or pain she found, or disappointment, she needed to learn the meaning of love. Never to rest, never to stop until she found it.

She told this to Ramar.

"Every creature you see in this meadow is a spirit," she said, "just like you and me. And we come here between our lives on earth to consider what living has taught us. That is how we grow, little by little, life after life, through what we learn."

Ramar was puzzled. "I do not remember the lives I have lived," he said, "so how will I learn?"

Lydia looked at him with love. "Well, you are a bit different," she told him. "Since you are a new spirit, you have never lived as a person. Instead, you have been blessed with a very great honor that happens just once or twice every few thousand years . . . the chance to bring the world some very great lessons it has somehow forgotten."

"You mean I will be born one day?" Ramar asked.

"Yes," said Lydia, "if you choose to be. Life is always a choice, as all things are. When you are ready to choose, you will know."

"What is it like to be born?" asked Ramar. It seemed a great adventure and he felt he was ready now.

Lydia tried to keep the smile from her voice because she knew his question was worthy of a thoughtful reply.

"What happens," Lydia told him, "is that when you are ready to be born you scrunch yourself up into a tiny speck of light, not even as big as the head of a pin. Then you concentrate on Earth and the people there, and before you know it, you will find yourself among them. Floating here. Floating there. Looking for the person you want to be."

Ramar listened intently as Lydia continued. "How will I know when I find him?" he asked.

"You will know," said Lydia. "You will find a tiny baby just newly born, less than an instant old, and you will know that he, or she, is meant to be you. It is a wonderful moment, I promise."

From the look on Lydia's face, Ramar thought it must be a beautiful experience to be born, and he wanted more than ever to be part of it. "What happens next?" he asked.

"Well, when you find the child that is you," Lydia continued, "you touch the baby's head until you sense a tiny spot on top that is not fully formed yet and you enter through there. Then, from that time on, you give the child life. You become all of its being. Its heart and its mind. Its thoughts and its feelings."

"Do I stay with the child?" asked Ramar.

"For all of its life," answered Lydia. "As long or as short as that life might be. Sometimes you live to be very old and sometimes for just a moment. It depends on what you need to experience or whom you have come to help."

"What happens when my life is over?" Ramar asked.

"You come back to the World-In-Between," Lydia replied. "You leave the body the same way you entered and you return to us as the light you were before. Once here, you rest for a spell and think about the things you learned in your lifetime. Later, when you are ready, you can choose to go back again if you wish and live as a different person. This way you just keep learning more and more and your spirit grows brighter and more fulfilled."

Ramar thought about this for the longest time. He understood some of what Lydia had explained, but not all of it. Too much was beyond him.

"Do not worry," Lydia assured him. "All that you need to know will unfold for you soon. The important thing is to never stop searching for the answers you want whether you find them in others or in yourself."

Just then, before Ramar could ask another question, he heard a fluttering sound around his head and a small white bird lit down beside him.

"Who are you?" he asked, surprised. "I have not seen you before."

"They call me the Dove Who Rhymes With Love," the little bird responded, "and I have come to help you, too." And with this, he laughed and laughed.

Ramar laughed as well because the dove was a happy creature and his joy was contagious.

"Have you been a person as well?" Ramar asked him politely, and the dove nodded yes.

"I have lived as a person many, many times . . . through needless trials and fruitless wars and pain that happened over and over."

"Then why are you so happy?" Ramar questioned. "It all sounds sad to me."

"Because I am a creature of faith," the dove replied. "I know that, no matter what has passed and gone before, peace will one day come. It will happen as soon as the world learns about love, and I have faith that one day it will."

"Faith?" asked Ramar. "What is faith?"

"I cannot tell you for sure," said Dove, "because it is something you feel without knowing why. Something you believe in because your heart says it is true."

Lydia laughed when she heard him. "This silly bird even believes that one day teeth will grow inside his beak so he can smile."

And Ramar laughed, too, in spite of himself. "Do you really believe that?" he asked his new friend.

"Indeed I do," the dove replied. "I know if I believe hard enough, and with all my heart, one day I will have a beautiful set of teeth, as white and beautiful as teeth can be. And when that happens, I will smile and smile so everyone can see."

Ramar understood how much the little bird meant it. He could see that of all the gifts the dove might ever earn, nothing could be so important or dear as the ability to smile and to express his love to others.

He could think of nothing so impossible, either.

But then again, what is more absurd than a rabbit with wings, he reminded himself. "Maybe there is something we can all learn together."

And Ramar was right, of course.

It was not by chance they had all come together in this World-In-Between. A rabbit with gossamer wings. A cat with aqua eyes and a Dove Who Rhymed With Love. You could sense there were bonds between them . . . gentle threads of feeling that no one could see or quite understand. Not even them.

But Lydia knew not to question or doubt. She had learned long ago that when you find a bit of magic in your life and you try to explain it, it sometimes goes away.

On Earth, they called it logic, she remembered, a need to explain or prove everything before you believe it. That was not unreasonable, she knew, but at the same time, there were so many things that logic had never told her. How do you explain love, she had asked herself. Or faith? Or friendship? And how do you tell people what imagination is, or how music happens or why poets hear what others do not?

It had often seemed to Lydia that the things she could not explain were surely as important as the things she could. Even more so.

Ramar heard her thoughts and he interrupted. He wondered what logic meant. "Has it something to do with being a person?" he asked, and Lydia replied that too many times it did.

She had learned that one of the perils of returning to Earth is that our senses change. We no longer hear what our spirits tell us or feel what makes us whole. We listen only with our ears, and see only with our eyes . . . and sometimes, even with all the natural gifts we have, we let others do our thinking. And make our choices. Or tell us how to live.

"Logic is something you reason with," she said to Ramar finally, "so once you are a person, you can decide if what you learn makes sense or not. The trouble is when logic is all you use, and you forget your intuition, you learn only part of the truth. It happens on Earth all the time."

It was an ancient lesson and Lydia knew it well.

There were so many things that Ramar would have to learn — things she wanted to teach him. She knew that he had come to change the world for those who would hear his voice and that she was to help prepare him.

She did not know how she would do this or what her part was to be. She knew only that Ramar was a child of creation as no other child could be. He was a rabbit with wings that no one knew the reason for. Not her. Not the dove. Not anyone.

Most of all, she loved him, and that was enough for now.

Two

I do not remember everything about those days in the World-In-Between, or when I lived them. Time is difficult to measure when you are away from Earth because days and weeks and years hold little matter.

It is the learning that's important.

I remember, too, because your spirit does not change; it does not age. It transforms from light to form to light again.

Lydia explained all that to Ramar.

She told him that all the creatures who lived in the World-In-Between were once human beings, most of them just recently. This was not their permanent home, she said. It is just that when a person dies, each may choose to rest here for a while . . . to think, to dream, to contemplate what they learned on Earth.

And one way to learn your lessons well, she told him, was to let your spirit be changed into the form of whatever creature you were like on Earth. You might become a cat. You might become a robin. You might come home as a puma or a peacock or a tapir or a spider.

"This part of the choice is never yours," Lydia explained, "and that is why the lessons are so important. The creature you become is a portrait of your real self," she said, "and once you understand it and know its lessons, you bring new growth to your spirit. That is what all of us want to do. It is our greatest purpose for being."

Ramar was not so sure about all that he was learning, especially the part he had heard about death. It sounded frightening and sad and he did not look forward to it.

"Will I die when I become a person?" he asked, and Lydia told him he would.

"Everyone who lives on Earth must one day die," she said, "but you should not be afraid because death is just like being born except in a different direction. You slip out of your body the way you came in, and soon you are back with all of us who love you. That is all that it ever is."

Ramar was satisfied with that, at least for the moment. The truth was his mind grew weary sometimes from all that he was learning, and now and then, some of it spilled from his head to be lost or forgotten. Or so it seemed.

But all the same, the days went by — or years perhaps — and Ramar and Lydia and the Dove Who Rhymed With Love grew closer and closer together. They became a trio that thought and moved as one, it appeared, as figures in a dance. First one would move forward and then the other, and then the other, weaving a tapestry of love and learning. Word by word. Thread by thread.

It was a marvel to watch them and all who passed near could feel the warmth that had grown between them, and they shared it, too.

Ramar was curious about everything and the more he explored and the more he questioned, the more he wanted to know. Most of all, he wanted to learn about the Earth, and where it was, and what it was like to go there.

And Lydia knew why.

She knew well that each of us grows and magnifies through our experiences as a person, not as a spirit. She explained to Ramar that we come to Earth again and again without a memory of the past so each life is new.

"You may visit Earth," she said, "for a hundred lives to learn just one important thing, or you may learn it in a moment and know it just as well. There are no rules or measures, and all the choices you make are yours. You are always responsible for what you do and feel and think. Both here and there."

Ramar wanted to be born and the sooner the better. "Am I ready now?" he asked. "Could I go today?"

Lydia told him he could if he chose to, but it might be better to learn the reason for his wings before he went to Earth. This might easily affect his choice, she said. The Dove Who Rhymed With Love suggested this as well, and Ramar agreed.

He decided to wait.

There was also the problem of missing his friends should he decide to be born. He would feel sad not to see them. Lydia. Dove. There could surely be no one like them . . . no one who would love him so much or that he could love, too.

Lydia understood the feelings because she had known them many times on both sides of life. "Each time we are born and each time we die," she explained to Ramar, "we leave everyone we love for a little while. It is not for long because friendships and families are part of forever, and we stay together from life to life and through all the times between."

Ramar was comforted by that. He hated to think of life without

Lydia or Dove. "You mean you will be born at the same time I am?" Ramar asked.

"I cannot say that," Lydia told him. "We cross back and forth at different times, and we look different, too, when we return to Earth. In one life you might be a man. In another life a woman. You might be black, or white or yellow or red, whatever you choose to be. The important thing is that you need to experience all that life is, and all it can be, before your spirit can return to light.

"You will understand more," she continued, "when you talk with others you see around you . . . for each has come back with a lesson that all of us can learn from if we take the time to listen."

And Ramar was always ready, of course, but he did not know where to start.

Lydia laughed and said, "You can begin by looking at your feet."

So Ramar looked down but he saw nothing but a small brown rock, lying between his paws as though someone had thrown it there. "I see only a rock," he replied. "Is that what you mean?"

"Look a bit closer," Lydia suggested, and Ramar bent down until his nose just touched the top of the stone. And then it moved, and Ramar jumped.

"It is a turtle!" Ramar exclaimed, and indeed it was. It was lying on its back, squirming to turn over, but its feet could not reach the ground.

When Ramar saw what was happening, he flipped him shell side up, and the turtle said thank you. "I have been lying here for a long, long time," he said, "hoping that someone would come. I was hungry and thirsty and frightened." And as he spoke, tears welled up in his eyes because he was not used to kindness or to being afraid, even as a person.

Ramar knew his pain as well. He had never seen turtle tears before, or any tears, for that matter . . . but he could feel them.

"Please do not cry," he said, touching the turtle gently. "We are all here to help you. My teacher Lydia, my good friend Dove, and my name is Ramar."

"I am called Micah," the turtle replied, and as he spoke, he struggled for memories that would not come back. He had forgotten who he was and where he had been and most everything else that mattered.

Lydia knew the feeling because she had made many journeys from Earth and awakened in the World-In-Between. "It takes some time to adjust," she said to Micah, "but you will remember things soon. I am sure of that."

But Micah was not. He was not sure at all.

It seemed he had been lying in his bed just a few hours earlier reading a story and . . . "Yes," he said, "I remember now. My eyes had grown tired so I shut my book, laid my glasses on the table, and turned out the light. Next thing I knew I was here on my back in your pathway, struggling to turn myself over."

"Your body died," said Lydia, "that is all that happened. The thing to ask yourself now is why did you live on Earth? What did you learn from your life?"

It all came back to Micah as Lydia spoke. A detail here. A memory there. His mother's face. A friend he knew in school. The dog his grandpa gave him for his fourteenth birthday. It all seemed distant now . . . just images and moments from a half-forgotten dream.

He spoke of what he remembered. The good times and those that were not so good.

The truth is that Micah had been a prideful man, strong and independent. "I never asked for help from anyone," he said, still proudly, "and I never gave any either. I lived my life as I wanted to live, beholden to no one."

"What about your family?" asked Ramar. "Do you not miss them and wish they were here with us now?"

"I did not have a family," Micah answered, "only my parents when I was small."

"Did you have friends?" asked Lydia, "people who loved you? They can be family, too, you know . . . closer sometimes than any other."

Micah answered that he did not have time for friends, that he had always worked and kept to himself. "I stayed out of everybody's business," he said, "and they stayed out of mine . . . and that is the way I liked it."

Ramar moved closer because the tears in Micah's eyes had not gone away. Most of all, Ramar sensed a loneliness about him as though an "empty spot" lived in his turtle heart that nothing had ever touched or filled. Not love or friendship or anything. Ramar wanted to fill it and take the hurt away.

Lydia said that in leaving his body on Earth, Micah had taken the form of a turtle so he would remember that the need of his spirit is to touch and merge with others. And this is true for all of us, she said, whether we are on this side of life or that one.

Lydia reminded Micah that during his time as a person, he had built a shell around himself and he had not let others touch him, and he had not touched them. And never had he shared his dreams, or his thoughts, or the hurts he felt. He had never asked for help, either — not once from anyone — even when he needed someone to care.

Lydia explained everything as best she could.

She said that as the years went by, and Micah did not change, his invisible shell grew thicker and thicker until finally no one could see the person inside — neither Micah the man nor his lonely spot.

"That is what happened," said Lydia. "Micah's shell became thicker and harder and his lonely spot bigger until the day he died." And that was just today, she said, before they found him.

The Dove Who Rhymed With Love understood, too, and after a couple of practice circles, he landed squarely on Micah's back and pecked on his shell as hard as he could. "It is like a rock," he told Ramar, "come feel for yourself."

But Ramar felt awkward, and he stayed beside Lydia, not moving.

"It is all right," said Micah, "you can touch me if you want to." And his voice was soft with feeling.

So Ramar touched him, and when he did, he felt a tremor that shivered through his body like a sudden chill. But it was not a chill. It was electric, and it touched him everywhere. In his mind. In his feet. In his ears. All in the very same instant.

The others sensed it, too.

It seemed to Dove and Lydia that for just a second, a shimmer of blue had passed through Ramar's wings when he touched Micah's shell. They could not be sure because it had happened too fast, and light can play tricks on your eyes, they knew, even in the World-In-Between.

They looked at one another and then to Ramar.

Ramar was different, it seemed. Not in an outward way or in any form that either friend could describe to each other. It was something they only sensed and knew to be true. Intuitively.

The truth is that in touching Micah's shell, Ramar immediately understood everything it meant, and the knowledge changed him. He knew the strongest need he would ever feel in body or spirit would be to touch and merge with others . . . to live in a ONENESS with everything around him. On Earth. In the World-In-Between. Wherever he might go or in whatever form he might exist.

He had learned the feeling of this already from his time in the meadow, but what he felt now was stronger and deeper because he had touched with Micah, and Micah's lesson was one he would never forget.

"Life is for reaching out to others," said Ramar aloud, "and for sharing what we are. Is that the lesson that Micah lived to learn?"

"It is something for all of us to learn," said Lydia, "because we all build shells around ourselves in one way or another. And while we needn't share everything we are and feel, we need the thoughts and ideas of others to help us grow. Just as we all need Micah and Micah needs us."

"And love," exclaimed Dove, joining in, "when we live without love, we live without everything — and that hurts most of all."

And so the day passed as the four of them sat down in the pathway and shared what they thought and felt in their hearts. Their dreams and ideas. Their hopes and disappointments. And except for Ramar, memories they carried from their days on Earth.

It was a time of learning, it was a time of love, and Micah's lonely spot that he had hidden for so long became smaller and smaller until it was gone.

Three

Ramar began to understand that everything around him held something he could learn from, and as they walked and talked and played together, Lydia showed him how true this was. Every hour. Every day.

"You can even learn from that little frog," she told him one morning, and she pointed to a small piece of sculpture half hidden by lilies near a small green pond.

It was a tiny gray frog, perfectly chiseled by a master's hand, and it rested on a mossy rock near the edge of the water. And its green frog friends jumped all around it . . . laughing, croaking, swimming in the water while Ramar watched them.

"What can I learn from a frog of stone?" thought Ramar aloud. "It cannot speak to me, can it?"

"Well, not in the way that you and I speak," Lydia told him, "but he can teach us something all the same, just by being here and letting us see him once in a while."

Then Lydia recounted the story that had once been told to her in the days when her spirit was as new as Ramar's and as eager to learn.

The frog had been chiseled, she said, from solid granite many lifetimes ago, the work of an ancient master. The master's name was Bahrue and he was uncommonly wise and gifted — so much so that his paintings and sculptures were admired and treasured by all who saw them.

"Bahrue was revered," said Lydia, "both for what he created and for his love of truth. And because he was thankful for the talent he had received, he spent much of his life trying to decide what great monument he could create in return for his gift. What could he leave behind for those who would follow? What great work of art? What magnificent sculpture? What could he say that spoke of life and how much he loved it?"

Ramar was all ears, and he and Dove moved closer as Lydia told them the story of Bahrue and the gray granite frog.

"Bahrue tried to create in stone what he felt in his heart," she said, "and his works became known throughout the world because of their beauty. Yet none seemed right or worthy of the monument he wanted to leave, and finally, in frustration, he laid his tools aside.

"Then, according to legend," Lydia explained, "Bahrue heard a voice in his heart and it told him to walk among the people of his city and to observe them in their lives, and that once he did this, he would know what gift he should leave behind.

"So Bahrue followed his heart," Lydia continued, "and he went out among the people, and he watched them and spoke with them and he learned about their lives — both those who were strangers and those who were friends.

"The years went by, and season followed season and day followed day. There were also those who followed Bahrue and sought his advice because he had proved himself both wise and caring, and they felt warm in his presence, as he in theirs."

"Was the granite frog his friend?" asked Ramar.

Lydia laughed at the interruption, and told him that frogs and people do not mix too well when they live on Earth together. "That only happens here," she said, "where we understand each other." Then she paused for a moment and went on with her story.

"Bahrue grew to be very old," she explained, "with a marvelous white beard that reached nearly to his waist and eyes that sparkled welcome to everyone he met. And though his hands were rough, and his clothing, too, he remained a gentle person with a strength not tempered by illness or time.

"He especially loved children," Lydia recalled, "and every day they would come to sit in his lap, and he would tell them stories, and share his wisdom and his laughter.

"Then one day a child brought him a small gray frog and laid it in his hand and the frog was dead. The boy, his eyes wet with tears, touched it with his fingers as it lay in the old man's palm.

"He asked Bahrue why his pet had died, and Bahrue drew him close in his arms and told him the story of a frog he once knew that could never make up its mind. It never knew which way to jump, he explained to the boy, unless somebody told him or helped him decide.

"Then one day, when all his friends were away, this little green frog sat alone by the pond, trying to decide which way to jump. There was a lily pad, all soft and green, that was just to his right, and a comfortable log that was just to his left . . . and both were tempting.

"First he would decide to leap to one, and then he would decide on the other, and then he would change his mind again — hour after hour. The sun went down. The moon came up. And the frog did not jump either way.

"In the morning when his friends returned, they found him in the same spot where they had left him, except now he was lifeless and gray. He had turned to stone.

"When his story was finished," Lydia said, "Bahrue smiled warmly at the boy in his arms. He knew at last that he had found the monument he wanted to leave for those who would follow behind him. It would be a small granite frog to remind us, through all eternity, that every path in life is a choice we must make for ourselves.

"Every person. Every life. Every day."

Lydia paused for a moment and touched the small gray frog that Bahrue had so masterfully chiseled as his gift for the ages. It was smooth and beautiful, created with a love that was still warm within it. Never to die.

"That is the lesson of the frog," she said to Ramar. "Bahrue created it to help us remember that no one can do our thinking for us, or make our choices, or decide what we should feel or do. We must always choose for ourselves."

"Always?" asked Ramar.

"Yes, always," Lydia told him, "because that is the way we grow, by thinking and choosing what we know to be right for ourselves even if others do not agree."

Ramar thought about that for a moment. "But do we not choose wrong sometimes?" he asked. "And do things we are sorry for later?"

Lydia laughed and Dove did, too.

"Of course," she answered, "we all make mistakes sometimes, but if we are afraid to be wrong, we can never be right, and deciding for ourselves is how we learn the difference."

Four

Ramar enjoyed his days with Dove and Lydia and together they explored the World-In-Between from one end to the other — the meadows and the mountains and the sands along the sea. They went everywhere as three who were one.

And for Ramar, especially, every day held something new to experience and learn — from the tickle of a caterpillar crawling along his nose to tracking through the mud by the edge of the river.

"Is the Earth the same as the world is here?" he would ask, and Dove and Lydia assured him it was.

"Well, except for the people," they would tell him, "but you will see that for yourself some day when you are ready to be a person."

Ramar thought often of the time he would journey to Earth and what kind of person he might become. "Does everybody get to choose who they will be before they are born?" he asked, and Lydia assured him again and again that they do. "Every spirit finds the child of its heart," she explained, "and when the search is done, they become that child as soon as it takes a breath."

Ramar liked that idea. "It must be wonderful to be born," he said, and Lydia and Dove agreed that it was. Then Lydia would turn to Ramar, and with that motherly look he had seen so many times, she would remind him that "every life is a time of learning and a time to treasure, but it is the learning that matters most."

"And learning to love," would echo the Dove, and Lydia would laugh and agree.

"It could be love that matters most of all," she would concede at times, but in her heart she knew there could be no difference — that love and learning are equal in their power to help us grow. She knew as well that nearly everything in life is a balance between one thing and another.

An ancient friend had told her — some eons ago — to remember a simple truth that he had learned through his many lives, and he had penned it on a piece of parchment to help her remember. When she read it, she found a short and mysterious lesson. All it said was:

The fish have flowers in them.

When she asked the meaning, her old friend touched her hand with his and told her that, just as fish is food for the body, flowers are food for the soul.

"Your soul gets hungry, too," he said, "just as your body does. You can fill it with friendship. You can fill it with laughter and music and with all the beauty you see in the world and there will always be room for more."

Lydia had kept this lesson in her heart from that time on and had passed it along to others as they crossed her lives. Now she explained it to Ramar and Dove as best she could.

"You will learn when you become a person," she said to Ramar, "that balance is what you grow by. You need to care for your body and your spirit both, though one is visible and one is not. And the same is true of the way you think and feel.

"If you think without feeling," she continued, "you will always have much to learn. And if you feel without thinking, you will lose the power that reason gives you, and the knowledge to change yourself and the world.

"Knowledge expands your choices," she explained, "as nothing else can."

Ramar was beginning to understand. In life there are things that your mind must search and answer, and others that your heart must feel and know. The question was how would he know the difference.

Lydia said maybe Dove could explain, and, flattered at the thought, the little bird folded his wings behind him and paced back and forth a bit, as thinkers are known to do. Finally, he paused and cleared his throat, and said in a hesitant voice, "I guess I don't know exactly."

Lydia chuckled softly to herself because she knew he would say that. He was not known for speaking out.

"Well, what do you think?" she asked him. "Just tell us your opinion."

Dove pondered again, a bit longer this time, then ventured his conclusion. "I think we should think with our hearts," he said, "in whatever we hope to learn."

"Precisely," answered Lydia, smiling. "That was not so difficult, was it?"

The little bird beamed with pride, for he had never been praised for his wisdom. It was his faith that he was known for — faith that he would one day grow teeth — and that was a dubious honor at best.

Ramar believed him, however, and Lydia — well, she had never laughed or said it could not be. She believed that every possibility deserved a hearing, even those her logic told her could never happen.

So her mind and heart were always open.

"The thing to be careful of," she cautioned her friends, "is that you do not live your life by what others think or believe unless you believe it, too. The choice is always yours and no one can take it away except for yourself."

She pointed to a cluster of palm trees to help reinforce her lesson.

"Look over there," she said, "and you will see the Reverend Smith, and right behind him is Father Christopher, I believe, and over to the left is the good Parson Goodbody. Each is a splendid example of what I mean."

Ramar looked across to the trees where Lydia had pointed, and what he saw surprised him. There in the heat of a steamy jungle was a trio of noisy penguins. They were running and moaning and chattering to themselves. They looked so out of place, he thought, three little creatures in their formal clothes, confused and frightened and sweating profusely.

He wanted to help them somehow, but afraid himself, he backed slowly away and closer to Lydia.

"On Earth they were called men of the cloth," Lydia explained, "and they devoted themselves to God and to saving the souls of others."

Ramar was puzzled and he looked at her quizzically. "Then why are they so frightened?" he asked. "Did they hurt people or do something bad?"

"Well, not intentionally," Lydia replied, "the truth is they tried very hard to do something good and to help those around them to grow. What they did not understand was that you cannot frighten people into thinking your way. They must always be free to choose and learn and believe for themselves."

That sounded easy enough to Ramar, but Lydia assured him it was not.

"It is a difficult lesson for each of us to learn," she told him, "but it may be hardest of all for those of the church . . . like Reverend Smith and Parson Goodbody."

"Why is that?" asked Ramar.

Lydia thought for a moment and could not find an answer that Ramar might understand. Finally she suggested he talk with the penguins and learn for himself, and that is what he did.

"Good morning, Reverend Smith," he said, introducing himself.

And the penguin replied, "Good morning." And so did Father Christopher and Parson Goodbody, though each was nervous and out of sorts.

"It is a little warm today, isn't it?" said Ramar, and the perspiring penguins agreed that it was.

"Actually, it is very hot," they replied. "Could you tell us where we are?"

Ramar told them they had come to the World-In-Between to think about their most recent lives and what they learned from their journeys on Earth. "Do you mean we have died," they asked, "and this is Heaven?"

"No," said Ramar, "this is not Heaven."

"Then is it Hell?" they asked, perspiring more freely.

"No," answered Ramar. "I do not know where those places are — not here, I am sure."

Lydia interrupted. "I'm afraid there is no Hell," she told them, "because none of us are punished for how we live or what we think . . . even for what we do."

"Of course, there is a Hell!" the penguins replied as one. "We all need to pay for the sins we commit. Everyone knows that."

"Yes, but how do we know?" asked Lydia quietly.

"It is in the Scriptures," they replied. "All of us must follow the Word of God or face the fire when we die. We have no other choices."

Lydia listened and smiled with understanding. "Then let me ask which is better," she said, "to follow something because you believe it is right or because you think you will be punished if you do not?"

The penguins talked among themselves for a moment, then Father Christopher said, "When you let people decide what is right for themselves, they may not choose correctly. It is better they know what can happen when a path is wrongly taken."

Reverend Smith and Parson Goodbody nodded in agreement.

"It is true," they said. "God has a plan for everyone and his will must be honored, always. He blesses those who follow his Word, and punishes those who do not."

Ramar had never been told about the one the penguins called God and he asked if he could meet him. The penguins told him that no person had ever met God because none was worthy enough. "Not one of us are," they said.

"He is holy and divine," said Father Christopher.

"He is Creator of all that is," said Reverend Smith.

"He is love," said Parson Goodbody.

"He does not sound like love," ventured Ramar. "Love does not punish people, does it . . . or make them afraid to think for themselves? God would not do that, would he?"

Just then, as Ramar spoke, a tremor of purple shivered briefly through his wings. It happened in just an instant, but Dove saw it and Lydia saw it and so did the penguins. And Ramar, though he had not seen it himself, felt the warmth of its light on his shoulders before it was gone.

All the creatures looked at each other and even Lydia was puzzled because she had never known anything like it. Not in all her lives or wisdom. "It must have something to do with why you are here," she said to Ramar. "A secret that will make itself known when it thinks you are ready."

"It could be a sign from God," said the Reverend Smith.

"Or from Satan," said Parson Goodbody.

"I think it was just the heat playing tricks on our eyes," said Father Christopher, though only the three were sweating.

"I am not warm," said Dove.

"Nor I," said Lydia. "We are all very comfortable here."

She understood why the penguins were sweating, though, and as they left them behind that evening, still pacing in the palms, she explained the reason to Ramar and Dove.

"The penguins," she told them, "now suffer the fate they promised to others because their promise was made in error. Your soul cannot be punished ever . . . on this side of life or the other. You either grow or not through the choices you make and what those choices teach you."

Ramar felt pity for the penguins all the same because he knew how unhappy they were. "Are not the penguins being punished?" he asked, because it looked so to him.

"No, it only seems that they are," Lydia answered. "The truth is that whatever we give to others, we also give to ourselves. If we give love to those around us, it comes back to us multiplied. If we do harm to others, that comes back as well, and many times over.

"What happened to the penguins is that as men of the church, the harm they did overwhelmed the good sometimes, in spite of their best intentions. They taught people to feel guilty and unworthy and this gave them sorrow and kept them from growing. They even described God as a tyrant father who demands to be worshipped and who threatens punishment for those who disobey him . . . and this made them afraid instead of loving."

"Then is it wrong to listen to what those of the Church might tell me?" asked Ramar.

"No, it is not wrong at all," Lydia replied. "A seed of truth exists in every church and every religion, and when those who follow that church return to the seed from which it grew, they will find its meaning again, and that is good."

Ramar thought about that for a moment but did not understand.

"If I one day listen to the fathers of the Church," he asked, "how will I tell which is closest to the truth?"

"The one closest to the truth," answered Lydia, "will be the one who helps you feel closest to God and how you come to see him."

"Is God not the same to everyone?" asked Ramar.

"In a way he is," said Lydia. "To some he is God. To some he is Allah. And to others . . . well, many just see him as Everything-That-Is. There is no one name that matters unless you think it does."

Ramar did not understand completely, but he knew that some day he would and he looked to Dove for reassurance.

"Do not worry yourself, my serious friend," said the Dove from above. "Your heart will take you where you need to go. You need only to follow . . . and listen."

"And have faith?" Ramar smiled.

"And have faith," echoed Dove, "but especially in yourself."

Five

Ramar wanted to learn about God.

He had heard Lydia describe him as best she could. He had heard the penguins speak of him, too. He even thought he could feel God inside his heart sometimes. He could not be sure. He only knew that of everything that existed in the World-In-Between, and in all the universes yet unseen around him, God must be the center of it.

He was part of it and all of it.

He asked Lydia if this was right and she said it was probably true. "Each of us feels God in a different way," she said, "so no one knows who is right or wrong or if it makes any difference. Whatever he is to you is all that matters."

Ramar was silent for the longest while. He did not see God as anything at all. He was neither a person nor a creature nor a thing, and yet he was all of these somehow — he was everything.

Lydia smiled as Ramar became lost in his thoughts. She interrupted gently. "Sometimes we see things more clearly when we have had some sleep," she said, and she suggested he rest for a time.

"I think we all should rest," said Dove, with a stretch of his wings, and with that, the three of them curled up together in the shade of an oak and were soon asleep.

Even a soft Spring rain could not disturb them, or the falling of the acorns or the scurry of the squirrels that scampered about them.

Ramar was especially tired and was sound asleep from almost the moment he closed his eyes . . . asleep and dreaming. And in his dream, he found himself still lying beneath the same giant oak, but Dove and Lydia were gone.

He did not know where they were or even that he was dreaming, and he called their names.

But neither answered.

Instead, there appeared before him an ancient man, the first human being he had ever seen. The man wore a woolen robe that was tattered at the sleeves and his long white hair fell down around his shoulders. Ramar would have thought him to be centuries old except he was spry and agile, with a light in his eyes that sparkled when he spoke.

"Good morning," he said. "My name is Bahrue."

Ramar had heard that name before, and he jumped to his feet as the ancient man approached him. "You carved the granite frog!" he said. "How happy I am to meet you."

Bahrue smiled warmly in return and the two sat down together and talked in a way that old friends do, instead of strangers.

"Do you remember what the gray frog learned?" asked Bahrue and Ramar answered he did.

"He learned that each of us must make our own choices," he said, "and that no one can make them for us, not even God."

"That is it exactly," said Bahrue. "But tell me — who is God and why does he matter?"

"I cannot tell you that," said Ramar. "I do not know who he is except I think he is everywhere, even here with us now."

Bahrue said what Ramar felt was true. "God is always with us because we are always with him. You cannot be separated from him any more than you can separate your left ear from your right one. What one ear hears, the other hears also. Especially ears as long as yours." He chuckled, and with that, he picked up an acorn and handed it to Ramar.

"The secret to God and to all of life," he said, "is in this little acorn, and if you keep it with you, you will always remember what the secret is and you will know what to do when your journey on Earth begins."

"Is it . . . magic?" asked Ramar, his eyes growing wide with wonder.

"In a way it is," said Bahrue, "because its secret could change the world when people remember and understand what I have told you."

Ramar looked at the small brown acorn, and he could see nothing unusual at all. It was simply an acorn like all the rest that lay around him. "Could you tell me the secret?" he asked Bahrue, and Bahrue said he would.

"But first," he said, "you must fetch me a stick so I can draw you a picture."

Ramar searched through the thicket as quickly as he could and returned to Bahrue with a strong oak stick and dropped it at his feet expectantly.

"Thank you," said Bahrue, "this is all I need."

Then as Ramar watched, the ancient teacher sketched a tree in the dirt and it was just like the one they were sitting under. A giant oak. Its top seemed to reach to the sky and its branches were thick with leaves, sheltering everything beneath them.

When that was done, Bahrue sketched in the roots of the tree and they reached as deep into the Earth as the tree stretched high.

It was a magnificent drawing and yet Bahrue sketched it so easily and naturally, it seemed the stick was a part of his hand and it carried his love to his art.

"There," said Bahrue, when he finished, "I have drawn you a picture of God, maybe the best I've ever done." Then he smiled contentedly, and put down the stick.

Ramar looked closer and he saw the giant oak that Bahrue had sketched for him. "Is God a tree?" he asked.

"I'll just say that God is like a tree," Bahrue replied, "and every creature is part of it. You and me and everyone. Every person ever born and every person yet to be."

Ramar looked at the drawing more closely. "Which part are we?" he asked.

"We are the leaves," said Bahrue, "and each time one of us is born and returns to Earth, we take our place on a branch of the tree and we stay there for life. Some choose a spot that is high and some choose a spot that is low, but wherever we exist, we experience life from a different perspective from anyone else in the universe and from any of our lives before. That is what makes every life we live so precious and unique."

"Does God know we are there?" asked Ramar.

"Since God is Everything-That-Is, he knows that each of us is part of him," said Bahrue, "just as you know your fingers are part of your hand. The thing to remember is that God is also a part of you as all of us are part of each other. No one is separate or alone."

"But why do we live on Earth?" asked Ramar. "And why do we keep going back?"

"We go back to bring knowledge to God," said Bahrue. "Every leaf, because it experiences life from its own special place, brings knowledge to the tree. For what the leaf sees, the tree sees, and what the leaf feels, the tree feels also.

"It is then true that what a person sees and feels, God also sees and feels and that is why we live. We contribute to God all that we learn in life and God learns with us."

"Then why do we die?" asked Ramar.

Bahrue looked down at his drawing and squinted his eyes for a moment, and as if by magic, all the leaves began to fall from his tree. One here. One there. Then more and more as Ramar watched them.

"We die when each of our seasons are through," said Bahrue, "just as the leaves must fall when winter comes."

"To be born again?" said Ramar.

"Yes," said Bahrue, "just as leaves come back to the tree."

The old man reached down and picked up his stick, and pointed to his drawing. "Each leaf that dies," he explained, "becomes part of the earth, and then part of the tree again. Then one day, when it feels itself ready, it appears anew — to experience life from a different branch and a different view than it knew before."

"Does it do this forever?" Ramar asked and Bahrue shook his head and smiled.

"Not quite," he answered. "One day when the leaf has learned everything it can, it transforms to an acorn and grows as a tree itself, with roots and branches and leaves of its own."

When Ramar awoke, the voice of Bahrue still echoed in his mind, and he wanted him back, if just for another moment or another word. But he knew that Bahrue had gone, and he opened his eyes to the morning light and saw that Dove and Lydia were stirring, too.

He also discovered that while he slept, a single acorn had fallen between his feet, which he took as a gift from his ancient friend. He didn't know for sure. He knew only that when he touched it, it was warm with love and wisdom and understanding.

He held the acorn for a moment and let its warmth flow through him. And when that was done, he walked to the meadow, away from the other trees, and there on a gently sloping knoll, with no one to see him, he buried his gift in the soft brown earth.

And no one knew except him and Bahrue.

Six

It is hard to measure time in the World-In-Between so no one knows how long Ramar and Lydia and Dove traveled and explored and learned together. Some say it was just a moment or two as time is measured here and others believe it was hundreds of years or more.

I'm sure it does not matter except to people who count such things.

But moments or centuries, I remember that I did not see the three every day, but when I did it seemed to me that Ramar was ever more wise and thoughtful. But he still loved to play, and often when he raced across the meadow, Dove and Lydia would watch from behind, as parents might lovingly watch their child.

Others would watch him, too, and occasionally he would stop and talk with them for a moment or two. He knew that every creature he met held an experience he could learn from — a lesson from their lives on Earth.

He met a swan who could not swim, a butterfly with pure white wings, and a pig with a light in its foot. And he came to love them all.

The swan was called Yolanda and her father had named her that before she was born, she said. "He told me I was the only flower in his garden." She smiled. "I did everything I could to please him."

"Is that how you spent your life?" asked Ramar, and she did not answer. It was clear that her memories, as distant as they were, still touched her with regret and disappointment.

Finally, in a low, wistful voice, she told her story.

"My father was a teacher," she said, "and a wonderful, warm, and compassionate man. I wanted him to love me and to make him proud of me by doing what he asked, so I followed in his footsteps."

"You were a teacher, too?" Ramar asked her.

"For nearly all my life," Yolanda answered, "but what I really wanted was to be a ballerina, and when I was growing, I practiced from morning until night, day after day after day. It was the happiest time I ever knew . . . but my father told me it was all just a dream, and would never be more."

"So it was not more," said Ramar.

"I never allowed it to be," Yolanda said. "And besides," she continued, "my dancing was important only to me and teaching was important to everyone. My father. The children. It was better that I chose for them."

Ramar thought about Yolanda for a long time after they met, and one day when he was walking with Lydia and Dove, he saw her by the riverbank, and she was sitting in the sun alone.

"Cannot all swans swim?" he asked of Lydia, and Lydia said they could.

"Well . . . as far as I know," she added, "because so many things change in the World-In-Between, you can never be sure."

"I know Yolanda cannot swim," said Ramar, nodding to his friend by the river, "and she is the most graceful swan I have ever seen."

And that was true. Yolanda was as naturally elegant as any creature in Ramar's world and he wished he could help her be happy.

"She will be all right," said Lydia. "She will soon remember that all of us have talents and gifts we are born with. Some have many such gifts and others just one, and the important thing is to use them. Otherwise, you lose them — like a swan who forgets how to swim."

"But is it not more important to teach than to dance?" asked Ramar, and Lydia shook her head no.

"Neither is more important," she told him, "because knowledge is food for the mind and dancing is food for the soul — and we need to nourish both."

Ramar had not remembered that. He had only thought of Yolanda and how she had wanted to please her father. "Is it wrong to listen to our parents?" he questioned. "And to do as they ask?"

"Of course it is not," said Lydia, "as long as we are children and need them to guide us. It is only wrong when we let anyone, even our parents, decide what we will do with our lives once we are grown. Only we can choose what is right for ourselves."

"Does it not matter that they love us?" asked Ramar.

"Love always matters," answered Lydia, "but to love your children is not to own them. You must let them be free one day to think and feel and to choose for themselves, as you must choose what is best for you. All people know this — they just forget."

Of all the things that Ramar was learning about life, the freedom to choose seemed by far the most important. In one way or another, he had heard its lesson from the gray granite frog, from the penguins, and from Yolanda and Lydia.

"How do I know I will always choose right?" he asked and Lydia explained that he would not.

"All you can do," she said, "is to follow whatever you believe to be right."

"And if others disagree?" said Ramar.

"Then listen," she replied, "and consider what they say."

"And if others laugh?"

"Ignore them," she said.

"And if I make a mistake?" asked Ramar.

"Then your mistake will teach you," said Lydia, "the same as all experiences do — both those that are good and those that are not."

"But there must be rules," said Ramar, "at least something to guide us in what we do."

"All you need to remember," Lydia answered, "is that whatever you give to others, you bring to yourself. If you hurt another person, or take what is theirs, the harm you do will come to you also, though many times over."

"And if I choose to help others?" asked Ramar.

"Then everything you give will return to you as well, multiplied in kind."

"Then should I not choose to do only good?" asked Ramar, and

Lydia paused for a moment, then smiled at him thoughtfully.

"That is a question only you can answer," she said, "because the only way you can grow is to make your own decisions."

"No rules?" questioned Ramar.

"No rules," said Lydia.

"I will not be punished, either?" asked Ramar.

"You will not be punished ever," Lydia promised, "no matter what you do."

Ramar glanced at Dove for reassurance. He felt that any lesson as important as this one could not be so easy to understand. It seemed much too simple.

"All truths are simple," said Dove. "It is only when we try to change them that we misunderstand."

And the truth, Lydia added, is that everything we think and feel and do in life either helps us grow or makes us smaller.

"The choice is always yours," she said to Ramar, "even when it seems that it is not. When you reach out with love and understanding and compassion for those around you, your spirit magnifies. It's like a light growing brighter. When you try to hurt others, or make them think your way, or take what is theirs, you diminish yourself and your light grows dim."

"Can it ever go out altogether?" asked Ramar, and Lydia explained that all people and all creatures have a splinter of light within them that is part of God; the light is their truest self.

"This God-part of you is always there," she said, "even when you or others cannot see or feel it. It is part of every person who lives even when it seems that no one loves you or even when the things you do are cruel and unworthy. There is still the light, and there is still its love to warm and guide you if you let it shine within you."

Dove knew this, too, and he shouted to Ramar to look far down the road at a small black pig who was rooting in the mud. "There," he said, "there is the light," and he pointed to the pig's hind foot. And it was true. Ramar could see it.

When the pig turned around just so, in just the right shadow, Ramar would catch a sparkle of light no bigger than a splinter and it gleamed from the pig's hind foot, as the flicker of a candle might shine through the darkness. And Ramar knew as he watched that the pig had never seen it, probably not once in all her lives.

"We never see the light of ourselves," said Dove, "because it is too much a part of us."

"Others might see it, though," said Lydia. "In the eyes of love sometimes. In a hand that helps. In a heart that will not give up. It shows itself from time to time in almost everyone around us — just often enough and long enough to renew our faith and promise."

Ramar understood about faith but not very much. He knew that Dove had faith that he would one day grow teeth so he could smile, but no one believed him. He was not even sure that Dove believed it absolutely but the little bird did. He believed it with all his might and with all his light.

Seven

Ramar never got tired of weaving the things he had learned into patterns of understanding — each idea and answer, each experience and each thing he felt. He wove them thread by thread in and around each other until they formed a tapestry of truth that grew clearer every day.

It was true as well that his wings grew larger as his mind grew more searching and open. There seemed a connection to Lydia — that his wings were somehow a measure of his learning and reflected what he had come to understand about life and living.

She could not be sure because she had never known a rabbit with wings, but Dove felt it, too. They believed, without knowing why, that Ramar had come as a gift somehow, not just for them or for the creatures who live in the World-In-Between.

Ramar was a gift for everyone — every spirit, every person, and every world we live in.

It did not matter how. It did not matter why. What mattered to Lydia and Dove was that they simply accept what he had become in their hearts and what they had become in his. So neither questioned more for now, or wanted to.

Lydia knew that her heart could recognize things that were plainly true sometimes even when her mind could not, and she told this to Ramar.

"You need always remember," she told him, "that knowledge comes from everywhere — in each thing you see and hear and experience, and in each thing you feel."

"Then what is the most important thing for me to learn?" asked Ramar. "What should I search for?"

"I do not have an answer for that," said Lydia. "I believe, though, that wisdom comes to those who learn to feel with their minds and to think with their hearts. It's the combination — love and thought together — that teaches us most."

Dove would have smiled had he only known how. After all, that "thinking with your heart" idea was sort of his, he recalled — at least in a modest way.

Lydia smiled as she remembered, too. "We all have the power to search and to think and to reason when we want to," she told him, "each for ourselves."

This meant Dove no less than Ramar, she explained. And Ramar no less than herself. And she no less than Bahrue.

"A turtle can learn to drop its shell," she said, "and a swan who's

forgotten can learn how to swim. And even a penguin, once he follows his heart, can do what helps instead of hurts.

"And the best thing," she continued, "is we do not have to live each lesson ourselves to understand it. We can learn from those around us."

Just then, as if by command, a flock of butterflies fluttered around Lydia's head, dancing as rainbows in the summer sun. Except for one. It was a large white butterfly that flew apart from the rest — a beautiful creature with huge pale wings. As the three friends watched it, it touched softly on Ramar's nose for a second, then flew to a spot right between his ears where it landed to rest.

Ramar turned his head stiffly so as not to disturb it, while Dove and Lydia watched in wonder.

"It looks like a crown," whispered the dove.

"It is a crown," said Lydia. "A butterfly crown."

And with that, they laughed together while all the butterflies disappeared, as quietly and quickly as they had come — except for Ramar's pale tiara. It stayed in its place between his ears, still and silent and barely breathing.

"Who are you?" asked Ramar, straining to see it.

"My name does not matter," the butterfly replied. "But you can call me Leonardo and I will answer to that."

"May I ask what you are doing on my head?" asked Ramar, and as Leonardo answered, he moved farther down on Ramar's forehead, to a place above and between his eyes.

"I am here to bring you a lesson," he said. "All you need to do is close your eyes and concentrate on the spot where I am sitting."

Then, before Ramar could say another word, Leonardo's touch turned strangely electric and the spot where he rested became as an eye for Ramar, a window for his mind to see through.

"Now concentrate," Leonardo urged softly, "and you will see a picture of Earth."

What Ramar saw first was the sky and the sky was blue, as he had seen it always. Then below the sky were clouds and they were blue also. Then he could see the Earth as it spun beneath the clouds and it was blue as well— the trees, the oceans, the land, and all the creatures who lived there. Everything was all the same color. No purple. No green. No yellow or brown.

"Keep watching," said Leonardo, and Ramar kept his eyes shut tightly so his vision would not disappear. Finally, each thing he saw returned to the color he knew it should be. The clouds became white again, as the snow on the mountains, and the forests returned to brown and green. And all the creatures became again as Ramar knew them in the World-In-Between. The redbird red. The elephant gray. The lizard a blue and yellow.

Then Leonardo asked Ramar to look at the people and to describe what he saw, and Ramar let his vision wander from one person and place to another. Slowly. Quietly. He took everything in.

"They are different colors, too," Ramar said as he watched them. "Some have skin of brown and some have skin of red and others of white or yellow."

"And what of their hair?" asked Leonardo. "Does every person have the same color of hair, or the same color of eyes?"

"No," replied Ramar, "these, too, are different."

"Now," said Leonardo, "let me ask you to look inside each person's heart, if you can, and to think as they think and feel as they feel."

Ramar was not sure how to do this, but he closed his eyes and imagined, and as he did, image after image flashed through his mind — like fragments of dreams that came and went before he could catch them. The dreams were not his and the thoughts were not his and there were words he had never heard spoken.

"You see," said Leonardo, "no two people are exactly alike in how they look or think or feel, or even in how they speak with one another. Each one is different, not as the rock is from the river but as the apple is from the pear and the lion is from the leopard.

"It is all of these colors and all of these creatures and all of mankind that make up the world that you will one day know — one day when you are a person."

"Will I remember all of this when I go to Earth?" asked Ramar.

"No . . . not in your mind," said Leonardo, stretching his wings as if to fly. "You will remember in your heart. Your heart will always tell you, if you listen, what your spirit knows is true."

"Is that the way people listen now?" asked Ramar.

"Some of them do," Leonardo replied. "A few here and a few there. Poets mostly and philosophers perhaps. Not many at all."

Then he stopped to reflect for a moment.

"Except," he continued, "there are those who keep the childlike part of themselves inside their hearts even when they are grown, and when difficult questions face them and they do not know what to do, that is where they look for answers first — inside their hearts."

"But should they not think as well as feel?" asked Ramar.

"Of course," said Leonardo. "We all need to think because that is what our minds are for. That is how we reason, and calculate and create ideas, and gain knowledge of the world around us. But just as Lydia has told you, it is important to listen to your heart and your intuition, too, because they will help you remember what your mind cannot see or hear."

Ramar could feel the wisdom in Leonardo's voice and the warmth of his spirit as he spoke.

But then, it seemed that warmth was everywhere, in everyone. It was part of Lydia and Dove. It was also part of Bahrue and Leonardo, and Yolanda and Micah, and even the penguins at times when they were not afraid and worried.

"Where does the feeling come from?" Ramar asked. "This warmth, I mean."

"It is from the splinter," Leonardo reminded him. "The same God-part within us that makes us worthy is the essence of love, and love is the essence of all that is. It creates. It inspires. It teaches. It tolerates. It heals and forgives, it —"

"It is also warm," Ramar interrupted.

"Ah, yes, it is warm," smiled Leonardo, "because its energy is the source of life. We exist because of love."

"And does love come in colors, too?" asked Ramar.

"The colors of love are as many as the minutes of a century," Leonardo answered, "with shades and hues that multiply their number yet many times again. You and I could never know or count them all, nor Lydia and Dove, nor all the creatures in all the worlds together."

Lydia nodded as she listened. "To understand love," she said to Ramar, "would be to understand everything, and no one has ever done that."

"Love is a mystery," said Leonardo, "that does not need an answer. It does not need anything, in fact. We just need to know that it is always there — within us."

With that, Leonardo flew from his spot on Ramar's forehead and made a whisper-soft landing on a blossom nearby. Then he looked at Ramar intently. "What have your visions taught you?" he asked. "Is there . . . say, one thing you have learned above everything else?"

But Ramar had no answer. "Not exactly," he replied.

He knew only that each and every thing — whether person, bird, or tree — is created in different colors, and all these colors together make up the face and hands and feet of God.

"That is it," he said to Leonardo. "It is not what's the same between us that matters . . . it is all the things that are different and how they fit together."

"You mean things are different from bird to bird?" asked Leonardo.

"Yes." Ramar laughed. "From bird to bird, from rabbit to rabbit, and even from butterfly to butterfly. Each of us is unique, if not in the ways we look and feel, then usually in the ways we think."

Leonardo was greatly impressed. "And what does this tell you?" he asked.

Ramar answered thoughtfully. "It tells me that I should always be sensitive to the beauty of others, and to hear each of them when they speak to me and to listen with an open mind."

"And what else?" asked Leonardo.

"It tells me that my way need not be their way nor their way mine," said Ramar. "We each have gifts that are ours alone and the more we share these gifts, the greater they multiply."

Leonardo interrupted. "You have learned all this just now?" he asked, ". . . just from your visions?"

"Well, no," said Ramar. "Some I have learned from Lydia and some I've learned from Dove, and Micah and Yolanda. And some is what the penguins taught me, and Bahrue and the gray granite frog. It seems to me there are lessons just about everywhere if we take the time to listen and think and remember."

Dove and Lydia looked at each other in mutual pride. "Our rabbit-friend grows wise," said Lydia, "and he speaks of truths that even ancient souls have somehow lost or forgotten — and truths that some never knew."

There was love in her voice as she spoke of Ramar, and there was a trace of sadness, too. She felt that one day — maybe very soon — he would be gone from the World-In-Between. She did not know how or why or when exactly, only that the time was growing near.

She turned to Leonardo, who rested yet on a blossom nearby. "What of Ramar's wings?" she asked. "Do you know their secret?"

Leonardo replied he did not, that in all his travels and all his lives and in all his gathered wisdom, he had never met or seen or heard of a rabbit with wings. Nor, indeed, had he ever known a rabbit like Ramar, even without his wings.

Ramar was unique in himself. There was no one like him.

Ramar did not hear them talking, though — either what they said or what they felt about him. His mind was caught in the colors he had seen. He knew that every creature and every thing and every thought and every feeling were like threads to be woven into his tapestry of truth . . . and life.

He thought of these as colors of love and he knew that in all those worlds where he was yet to travel there was a place for each and every one of them. Each creature belonged. Each thought was valid. Each feeling. Each choice. Each color. There was nothing meant to be apart or alone.

He also knew that when he became a person, he would be free to think and choose for himself, and it was the only way that he could grow. Should he have a destiny, he thought, it would be to search for truth, as it is for all who live with an open heart and an open mind. And the promise he made was that he would listen through both as best he could, today, tomorrow, and always.

It was just at that moment, as the promise was given, that he felt a stirring in the pit of his stomach he had never known before. It was small at first and he hardly felt it. But then it grew stronger and it spread through his chest, and then to his head, and then to his wings — gaining power as it grew.

Again, it seemed something electric — an energy in itself — and even Lydia and Dove and Leonardo could see and hear it as Ramar's wings began to tremble with its coming.

Others could sense it, too, and they came forward as well, some by twos and some by threes and some alone, and they watched in wonder as Ramar's gossamer wings exploded into rainbow wings of light — bright and magnificent and brilliant with color. There were reds. There were greens. There were blues and purples. There was nothing so beautiful in all the world.

And Ramar was different, too. There was now a splendor about him — a wisdom and a warmth, some thought, not there before. They saw it in his eyes when he looked their way and heard it in his voice when he spoke.

"What has happened?" he asked, as he looked in the faces around him, and no one could tell him. Not Lydia or Dove or Leonardo. Not anyone.

"None of us can say," they told him, "for it is not in our knowledge. We can only wonder and wait for the answer, as you must do."

They could say no more.

Eight

The news of Ramar's transformation raced quickly through the World-In-Between until all had heard about it. Some believed it and some did not.

"It is the work of the Devil," said the penguins, "for a rabbit to have wings in the first place." And with that, they nodded and chattered among themselves, still perspiring as before.

"It is merely a trick," said others. "And a sham," said some.

But those who knew Ramar had neither question nor doubt . . . not for a moment. They knew that his wings were genuine, alive and aglow with all the colors of the universe — with warmth, with love, with compassion and understanding.

They could feel only love for him, and should there be questions about his wings, the love was answer enough. They gathered around him and they touched his wings gently as one might touch a thing that is sacred. And the touch gave them a share of his knowledge, too, and a sense of belonging to something greater than themselves and what they were before Ramar came.

Ramar understood their longing and he walked among all the

creatures who came to see him, and he shared their joy and the lessons of their lives, and he sought to help them and to answer their questions.

And all the while, Lydia and Dove and Leonardo never left his side because they, too, wanted to help and to be close to their friend. Each of them knew that one day soon Ramar would leave them for his first life on Earth — and while that was a mission that all must answer, and they knew that as well, it did not diminish the sadness they felt.

The questions were many. When would his life on Earth begin and who would guide him to the place he belonged? But no one knew, least of all Ramar. He knew only that he was tired and he wanted to rest, alone perhaps, and away for a time ... even from those he loved.

The place he yearned for most was the meadow where he had first appeared on that warm spring day in the hollow log that was home. It seemed so long ago. Yet everything about it was as fresh in Ramar's mind as moments just past.

He knew each rock, each nest of clover, and he could smell the grass and the warm brown earth from which it grew. He wanted to go there because if there was an answer to the riddle of his wings, and why he bore them, he would find it there.

So, knowing this, he left his friends and returned to his childhood home. "I will just be a day or so," he told them. "Not more than that, I promise."

Once home, he found the hollow log where he had slept as a young, growing rabbit. It seemed so small now, but even so, it had weathered well and could serve as a pillow for a rabbit now grown.

So Ramar fell asleep, his head against his favorite log, and as he dreamed of his younger days, his magnificent wings folded around him and covered him like a blanket, glistening in the afternoon sun. Evening came, and still he slept, and then through the night and the morning.

Finally, late on the second afternoon, he was awakened by a strange kind of silence around him. He knew, without opening his eyes, that nothing was moving, neither squirrel nor chipmunk nor mockingbird. Even the wind he loved made not a sound, and the crickets held their songs inside themselves as though waiting for something to happen. Or for someone to come.

He did not know which it would be, but when he opened his eyes, he saw a radiant white lamb approaching from the distance — a lamb with two red feet. He had come down from the hillside, far beyond the meadow, and he walked with a grace that Ramar had never witnessed in any other creature.

Ramar saw, too, that the creatures of the meadow walked and crawled and flew about the lamb as though he were a prince or teacher, and occasionally he would stop and speak with one of them. Ramar could not hear what they said, but he could feel the reverence that every creature held for the lamb. They loved him. They loved him more than they loved themselves, he thought, or life itself.

Ramar watched as the lamb came nearer and he marveled at his beauty. "How could such a creature exist?" he asked himself. None could be so pure as he, or hold such wisdom or emanate such love. Ramar was sure of that. He was also sure that whatever waited ahead for him, whether life on Earth or something else, the lamb would be part of it always.

Their souls were connected — linked in a way he could not describe or prove to himself, but which he knew existed. That was all that mattered.

"Good evening," said the lamb when he reached the spot where Ramar waited. "I have heard of you and your rainbow wings and I have come to meet you."

His voice was warm and as familiar as that of a longtime friend, and yet Ramar had never heard it before. "My name is Ramar," the rabbit replied, and as he spoke, he instinctively lowered his head as though bowing before someone more worthy than he.

The lamb felt awkward. "I am not more worthy than you," he said, sensing what Ramar felt. "I am whatever you are — no more, no less, just different."

"But who are you?" Ramar asked, "Have we met before?"

The lamb folded his legs and sat down on the grass. "I have been called by many names," he said, "but none of them really matter. Some call me The Shepherd now."

Ramar could not help but smile. "A sheep who is also a shepherd?" he asked.

"Yes," said the lamb. "For life has taught me that each of us must learn to care for ourselves, and to care for ourselves, we must also care for those around us. Thus I am a sheep and also a shepherd."

Ramar could feel the wisdom of this clear through to his bones. He knew The Shepherd was not like other creatures. It was not that he looked so different except for his two front feet, which were crimson red, and his eyes, which were crystal blue. There was something else about him, too, something that Ramar could sense but not describe so he did not try.

It seemed to Ramar that The Shepherd, like Lydia, was neither young or old, but a timeless creature, childlike at times when he spoke of love, and ancient at times when he spoke of truth. Ramar felt good being near him. He didn't know why, but he believed that if he cut himself on a twig somehow, The Shepherd could touch the spot where it hurt and the hurt would go away. It would bleed no more.

And this was true.

He also believed that if he hurt inside and his heart was heavy with grief and disappointment, The Shepherd could touch him there as well and his heart would lift itself and sing.

And this was true.

He also believed that if The Shepherd wanted to leave the meadow and walk across the pond without sinking beneath the water, he could probably do it — as easily as Ramar could walk across the grass.

And this was true.

There was nothing that Ramar could ask of The Shepherd that was not in his power to grant. No question, it seemed, that he could not answer. And yet, with all his power and wisdom, there was a warmth about him that transcended even these — and the warmth was love.

Some of what Ramar sensed in The Shepherd was what other creatures now sensed in him since he had gained his rainbow wings. So in all these ways — in their warmth and their love and their wisdom — The Shepherd and Ramar were quite alike. Some even thought them anointed, destined to become as one.

Ramar asked The Shepherd if he knew the secret to his rainbow wings, and The Shepherd answered that would he think about it Ramar would find the answer for himself.

"I will tell you this," The Shepherd said. "Each color in your wings embodies a single truth for you and others to see and remember."

"Can you tell me these truths?" asked Ramar.

"I can tell you to look for yourself." The Shepherd smiled, and Ramar turned to look at his wings as best he could, folding them forward as far as they would reach.

He looked first at the blue and it seemed like a window that let him see beyond where he was and what he knew. He understood immediately that truth is not a static thing like a wall or a rock or a rule. Truth is a window that opens our minds to new ideas and discoveries and maybe, most of all, to changes and choices.

"Truth is a growing thing," he said to The Shepherd and The Shepherd agreed he was right.

So, one by one, Ramar peered carefully through all the colors of his wings — the reds, the greens, the purples, all of them — and as he did, he remembered what he had been taught by those he had met.

Through the blue, he remembered the turtle, Micah, and the shell that had grown around him because he had not shared himself with others — nor touched with others or let others touch him. "Is one of the truths that we grow by sharing ourselves and our ideas with others?" he asked, and The Shepherd said it was.

"Are all truths as simple as that?" asked Ramar.

"As simple as that," The Shepherd answered, "because the essence of what is true is something that never changes, only grows. We can live alone and think only of ourselves or we can share what we feel with others. And the more we share, and care, the closer to grace we become."

"But what is grace?" asked Ramar. He had not heard of grace until now.

The sheep who was also a shepherd explained that grace is knowing a ONENESS with the Everything-That-Is. It is how our spirits feel once we have lived all our lives on Earth and understand all the lessons now crystallized in Ramar's rainbow wings.

"Are there many who have known this ONENESS?" asked Ramar.

"Just a few," said The Shepherd, "and that is all."

Ramar remembered the penguins and what they had told him. "The penguins believe that God will punish those who do not do as he asks," said Ramar. "Could this be true?" It was something that sometimes worried him still.

"No, you cannot be punished by something you are part of," The Shepherd replied. "Each of us is free to shape our lives in any way we choose. Should there be punishment, it would take away our choices, and should we not have choices, we could not learn or grow to grace."

"But what of the sins the penguins described?" asked Ramar. "Can we do what is wrong and not be punished?"

"Who is to punish you?" asked The Shepherd in return.

"God would punish me," Ramar ventured. "That is what they told me. They said that most of the world believes this is true. Should I not listen?"

"Can your right hand punish your left hand?" The Shepherd asked. "If you remember the splinter of light you saw, you will know that God is not separate from you but part of you. This means to fulfill the promise of life you must live it without fear, and you must follow your own free choice in all things — not hurting those around you or imposing your will upon anyone else. If there be sins, then these are sins. No others."

"You mean it is wrong to ask others to believe as I do, if what I believe is true?" asked Ramar.

"It is only wrong to force them," the Shepherd replied, "or to interfere with their choices. When you do this, you interfere with their growth and bring harm to yourself as well — just as you do should you hurt another or take what is theirs."

Ramar remembered what Lydia had told him. "Each thing you give returns to you in kind," she had said. "Give love and it comes back to you multiplied, again and again. Do harm and it comes back as well, though many times over. In this way, it is you who chooses your fate by what you think and feel and do. You and no one else."

Ramar had believed his friend completely and yet, when all these same words were spoken by The Shepherd, they reached into his heart and became part of him. He understood them in ways that he had not understood before, as though he had lived them.

"Each color of your wings is a color of truth," reminded The Shepherd, "and is now a part of your spirit so you may teach these lessons to others when you are born as a person."

Ramar was not sure that he knew the lessons well enough to serve as a teacher, or that he even knew how. He was not a teacher, or a minister, or a spirit of great wisdom. He had not even been a person yet.

"It will be difficult," said the Shepherd, "but I can tell you it is the childlike mind that sees the truth and the open mind that receives it. If you center yourself in the lessons you have learned, the words to teach them will fall to you as naturally as rain will fall on an emerald land. You need only have faith . . . and listen."

"But who will listen to me?" asked Ramar.

"A few will hear you," said The Shepherd, "maybe only one or two. Just remember that once it is said, truth reaches out to those who need it, and those who need it are many."

With that, The Shepherd reached over and kissed young Ramar softly on the cheek as though bestowing a blessing upon him for those times when he would need it. "Is this good-bye?" asked Ramar, and The Shepherd told him it was. And with those words, Ramar felt a sadness within him as though his heart would wither and die, and tears so filled his eyes that he could not see.

"Please," he said to The Shepherd, "if I go to be born as a person, could you not go with me and help me teach what we have learned?"

"I cannot go with you," The Shepherd replied. "I can only tell you that once when I went to Earth, as you will go, I spoke of the things that we have learned and I taught them in parables and stories. Then one day when my lessons angered those who believed in a different way, they nailed my hands to a cross of wood and there I died."

Ramar looked down at The Shepherd's crimson feet and his sadness was multiplied. It was a sadness that overwhelmed him.

The Shepherd looked into Ramar's face, and he was moved by the tears that fell from his eyes. "Do not be sad, my rabbit friend," he said, "for many have gone to Earth as I have gone. There was Moses . . . and Muhammad . . . and Buddha . . . and the Shawnee Prophet. I cannot name them all. I can only tell you truth is found in many faces behind many eyes and you must always be ready to see it."

"Do they remember you yet?" asked Ramar, "or has everyone forgotten?"

"They speak of us all," The Shepherd replied, "and there are some who call to us and who pray to us, and who build churches in our names, and we are both honored and disappointed."

"But how could one who is honored be disappointed?" Ramar asked him. "Is honor not love in its way?"

"Of course," replied The Shepherd, "but I am honored for many things I did not say or believe and for many events that never happened. Because of this, my words and my lessons have been lost and forgotten, as have the words of many. I know it is time to speak them again."

"But I do not want to leave you," Ramar said, and there was pain in his voice, and sorrow in his heart.

"Do not be sad," said The Shepherd, "for all who live will die and all who die will live again. And all who are friends will always be friends and never part. Love holds us together for always."

Ramar was comforted by that, but not completely. "If you cannot go with me, maybe you could guide me," he said, "and that would be all I need."

"Then I will help guide you," The Shepherd agreed. "When you are born, part of me will go with you, and when you think of me, you will feel me inside you. And when you need my help or counsel, I will whisper in your ear and your heart will hear me. I promise you that."

Ramar was then content because he knew that whatever journeys were his to make and whatever hardships were his to conquer he would not be alone.

"It will soon be time for you to go," said The Shepherd, and Ramar said that he was ready, except he wanted to see his friends for just a moment to say good-bye.

So with that, they left that part of the meadow where Ramar first came to be, and they walked together, side by side — a rabbit with rainbow wings and a lamb with crimson feet — to the place where Ramar knew his friends were waiting.

Nine

As Ramar and The Shepherd walked through the hillsides of the World-In-Between, a host of creatures gathered behind them. There were giraffes and fireflies and reptiles and eagles — every creature ever created.

Those who were weak were helped by those who were strong, and those who could not see were led by those who could. And those who were few became a crowd, and the crowd became a throng, and yet they were hushed and still.

No creature spoke or sang its song.

Finally, from the crest of a sun-lit hill, Ramar could see his old friends waiting for his arrival. Lydia was there, as poised and as regal as ever, and Dove flew around her head in such perfect circles they seemed a giant halo for one who is holy. Leonardo was with them, too, his pale wings spread above him like the sails of a ship on a sea of green.

They were beautiful to see and they filled a spot in Ramar's heart that had felt empty since he had left them. He trembled with joy, and called their names as he ran toward them. "Lydia! Dove!" he shouted, and they turned their heads to see him and their eyes lit up with love.

"I've come home again," called Ramar, and he ran so fast that his rainbow wings lifted him gently into the air and he soared above everyone's head for more than a moment, even higher than Dove and Leonardo. Then he set himself down in front of Lydia.

"Oh, how we have missed you," said Lydia. "It is good to have you back again."

"Yes, and I have found a new friend," said Ramar, "a sheep who is also a shepherd."

"We have learned of The Shepherd," Lydia told him, "for he is known through all the worlds of all the universes and through all the dimensions of space and time. He has been many times a prophet and a shepherd to us all."

It was at that moment, well behind Ramar, that the lamb arrived, and Dove, Lydia, and Leonardo could only gaze at him and feel the wonder of what he was. No one spoke. Not The Shepherd. Not Ramar. Not anyone. There was too much feeling between them to let words interrupt — at least for a moment.

Finally, Ramar broke his news to Lydia. "I am soon to be born," he told her, "and The Shepherd has said that he will be with me and he will help to guide me through all the days that I live on Earth."

"And what will you do with those days?" asked Lydia.

Ramar answered in an instant. "I will be a teacher," he told her, "and I will share the lessons of my wings with all who wish to hear them."

"And what are the lessons?" asked Leonardo, and he and Dove and

Lydia moved closer to hear, as did all the creatures who had gathered about them.

Ramar could not answer right away because what he had learned was hard to put into words. He felt the lessons were not so much for saying aloud or writing down as they were for feeling. Once you sensed them and held them in your heart, you would know the meanings, and the meanings would change you forever.

Teachers do not teach that way. Ramar was sure of that. Nor students listen.

He spoke to Leonardo.

"I will tell those who hear me that we cannot love each other unless we first love ourselves, and we cannot judge one another unless we are willing to be judged as well. Nor can we do harm to others without harming ourselves, or think for another, or choose for another, or force anyone else to think and live as we do."

"But what if all you bring to the world is truth?" asked Leonardo. "Should those around you not listen to what you tell them? And if they don't, should you not force them?"

"Wisdom cannot be given to those who do not want it," Ramar replied. "It can only be received. And those who receive it must first choose to hear it. There is no other way."

Leonardo smiled in admiration. "You have become most wise, my precious friend," he said. "Is this what The Shepherd has taught you?"

Ramar smiled in return. "Yes," he answered. "I have learned from The Shepherd as I have learned from you and from every creature I have met."

"Then what will you say when they ask you about what God is?" asked Leonardo. "Have we taught you that?"

"I will say that God is Everything-That-Is and we are all a part of him . . . just as the leaves of an oak are part of the tree, neither separate from it or from one another."

Lydia interrupted. "That is a very hard lesson to learn," she said, "and few will believe it. Perhaps not a soul in all the world." But Ramar believed it. He had seen the pig with the light in his foot and he knew that the light was God.

"But we each have a light within us," he said, looking to The Shepherd. "I am sure that is true."

And The Shepherd agreed that it was. "It is no bigger than a splinter," he said, speaking to the crowd now gathered about them, "but that is big enough if the splinter is God."

He beckoned to the Dove Who Rhymed With Love.

"We must have faith in ourselves," he said, "and know that God is within us, each one . . . even the most humble of creatures and the least of mankind. And in those times when it seems that the splinter is gone and hidden from our eyes, we must still believe it is there, as fully and faithfully as Dove believes he will one day grow teeth."

Dove blushed as The Shepherd spoke. He was not used to such attention, certainly not from one so revered as the sheep who was also a shepherd. If he could smile, he would have smiled, but of course, he could not — at least not yet.

Ramar had listened intently to each word The Shepherd said, for it seemed that his own heart was speaking instead of the lamb. He could not explain it, or understand it. He knew only that the wisdom of The Shepherd lived in his own heart as well and that he would one day share it with all who would listen.

The Shepherd got up from the place where he sat and stood beside Ramar. "I think it is time to go," he said, "if you think you are ready."

"I am ready," said Ramar, and as he answered, there was a glow around his wings and each bright color shimmered with the warmth of light.

Suddenly he knew the meaning of his wings and why they were his. He looked to The Shepherd and The Shepherd knew as well. "Truth gives you wings to ONENESS with God," he said to Ramar, and there was a grace in his voice that removed any doubt.

Ramar was certain now of every lesson he had learned. His only question was how could he remember them all when he was no longer a rabbit with rainbow wings. "Do people remember what they have learned in the World-In-Between?" he asked, and The Shepherd told him they sometimes do.

"You will not remember everything at first," he said, "but little by little, as you live as a person, it will all come back to you — each color, each lesson, each reason for being."

Ramar was satisfied with that. He was ready to be born. He would hold the lessons in his heart as best he could, knowing that he was not alone.

But how could he say good-bye, he wondered. What would life be without Lydia and Dove and Leonardo? They were as dear to him as life itself. And knowing this, he looked at them lovingly, one at a time, etching their faces in his mind and memory so he would never forget them.

Lydia felt a sadness, too, for she had come to love Ramar with all her heart, and he could see it in her eyes as he searched her face for something he might have missed. And Dove, sensing the moments to come, looked the other way when Ramar came near so he would not see his tears. Dove had faith in the future and what was to be . . . but today, all he could feel was the pain of parting. Ramar would soon be gone.

And finally, there was Leonardo who, for once, said nothing at all because he knew his voice would give away his feelings should he try to speak. His wisdom was one thing, but his love was quite another — too deep for good-byes.

"Is this what death is like?" Ramar asked them and Lydia found words to answer.

"A little," she told him. "It is always sad to leave the ones you love even when you know the parting is not forever."

"Only life is forever," reminded Leonardo, "and death is for just a moment. That is something to remember always."

Ramar was satisfied with the truth of that, but not entirely, and tears rolled down his cheeks as, one at a time, he kissed his friends good-bye. Beautiful Lydia. Faithful Dove. Thoughtful Leonardo. "I will see you again," he said, "even before you know it."

And with that, as the rest of us gazed in silence, Ramar glanced lovingly at The Shepherd for one last time, then rose through the clouds on his rainbow wings until he was out of sight.

Then, in the darkness, while all of us still watched our good-byes, there came a light from above our heads. It was small at first and only a few took notice. But then as it dipped and looped and circled above the crowd, it grew brighter and brighter until it shone on everyone. Every face reflected its glow and every soul its glory.

It was the gleam from Dove's new teeth.

A Word from the Author

*Often when I think of Ramar, I am not entirely
sure if my memory of him is from the past or
from the future. These "loops of time" I mentioned
have always been a mystery to me. I would not be
surprised if I drift around in a circle sometimes
and do not even know it.*

*My memory of Ramar remains vivid all the same, and
in my mind's eye, I can still see him rising through
the clouds — his magnificent crystal wings glistening
above me in rainbow bursts of color and light.*

It is not a thing a person forgets.

*Actually, I am reminded of Ramar nearly every day
in one way or another, and while I have not yet
seen him in anyone's eyes, I am almost sure he
is here — living among us or within us somehow.*

*I hear him in my heart as Ramar must still
hear The Shepherd.*

But even if his voice were still, I know what
Lydia and Dove and Leonardo would say
if one day I questioned my feelings or
doubted what Ramar has taught me —
so I can never lose faith.

All I can do is write what I remember,
and this I have done.

I should tell you, though, from time
to time I still catch a glimpse of
that in-between world and all the
creatures I came to love.
It can happen in an instant,
when I least expect it — in a word,
in a song, in a smile or a touch,
or through a random recollection
that makes itself known when
it thinks I am ready.

In these and in dreams,
I go back again —
and I know
wherever my
choices take me,
there will always be
a splinter of light
inside me that can
never be diminished.
It is a light that
lives and shines
in each of us,
in every person
and every creature,
that nothing can
drown or smother
or take away.
Not life.
Not death.
Not even ourselves.

I learned that from Ramar
and I know it is true.